Little Lucy

small and shy

Published by:
Crossbridge Books, Worcester
www.crossbridgeeducational.com

ISBN 978-1-913946-75-3

End plates by Shaun Wilkinson

Little Lucy

small and shy

Written and illustrated by

Ann Goddard

For Hannah and Jennifer

Little Lucy
small and shy,
shy and small,
hides her face from all.

Always alone, no friends at all,
but friends with birds
in the woodland tall.

Plate 1

In the beginning God created the heavens and the earth. *Genesis 1:1*

Then God said... "Let birds soar above the earth in the open expanse of the heavens." *Genesis 1:20*

One day little Lucy found a stone.
A special stone,
bright and shiny, shining bright,
her face reflected in the light.

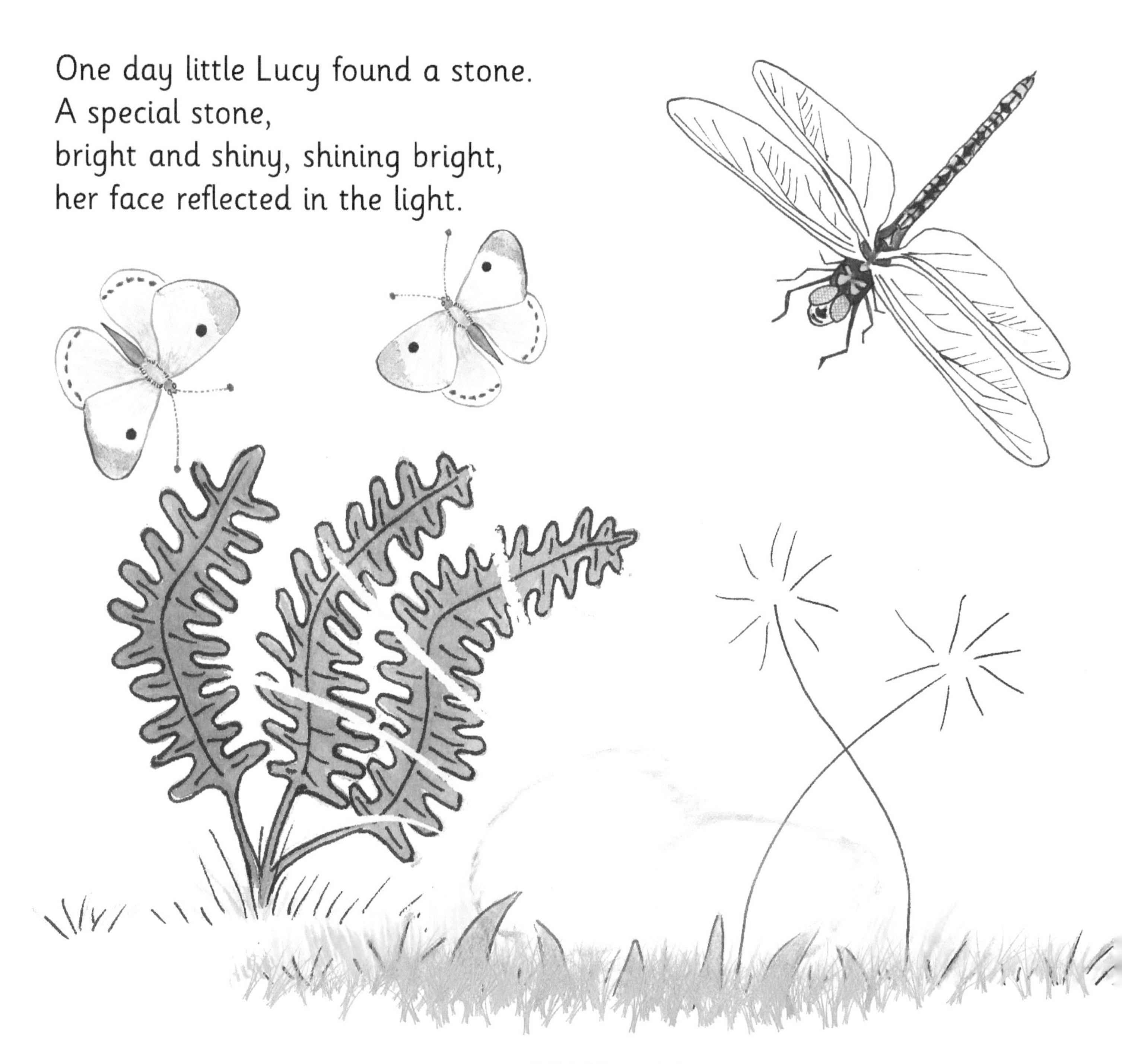

"Oh!"said Lucy, "How beautiful."
The stone seemed to whisper in her hand.

Magpie flashed by,
black and white, white and black.
She swooped and shrieked,
and snatched the stone from Lucy's grasp.

"Oh!" cried Lucy.
"Magpie stole my stone, my special stone
that's bright and shiny, shining bright."

Little Lucy, small and shy, shy and small,
hiding her face from all...

stood UP.

“Time to be BIG not small,
time for adventure,
to be brave, to take control.”

So off she went...

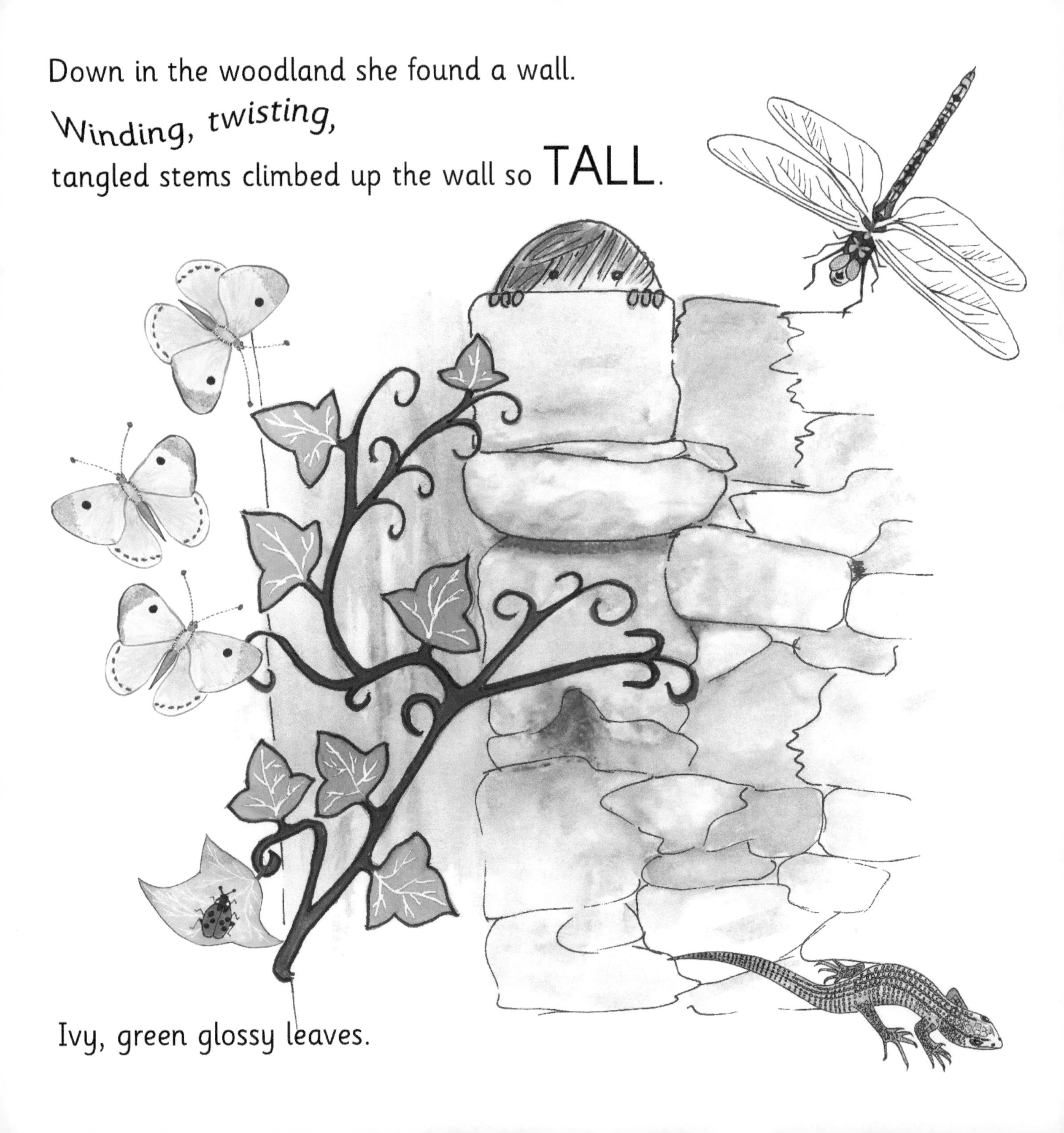
Down in the woodland she found a wall.
Winding, *twisting*,
tangled stems climbed up the wall so TALL.
Ivy, green glossy leaves.

Little Lucy moved the leaves aside
and there... A NEST.
Woven together, twig upon twig,
a grassy cup.
Far too tiny for Magpie.

Small and brown, with red breast, was Robin
hopping from branch to branch.

Lucy sighed and said, “Oh Robin!
Magpie stole my stone, my special stone
that was bright and shiny, shining bright.”
“It’s little Lucy!” said Robin.
“I remember you. Take one of my red feathers.
If you need me, I will come.”

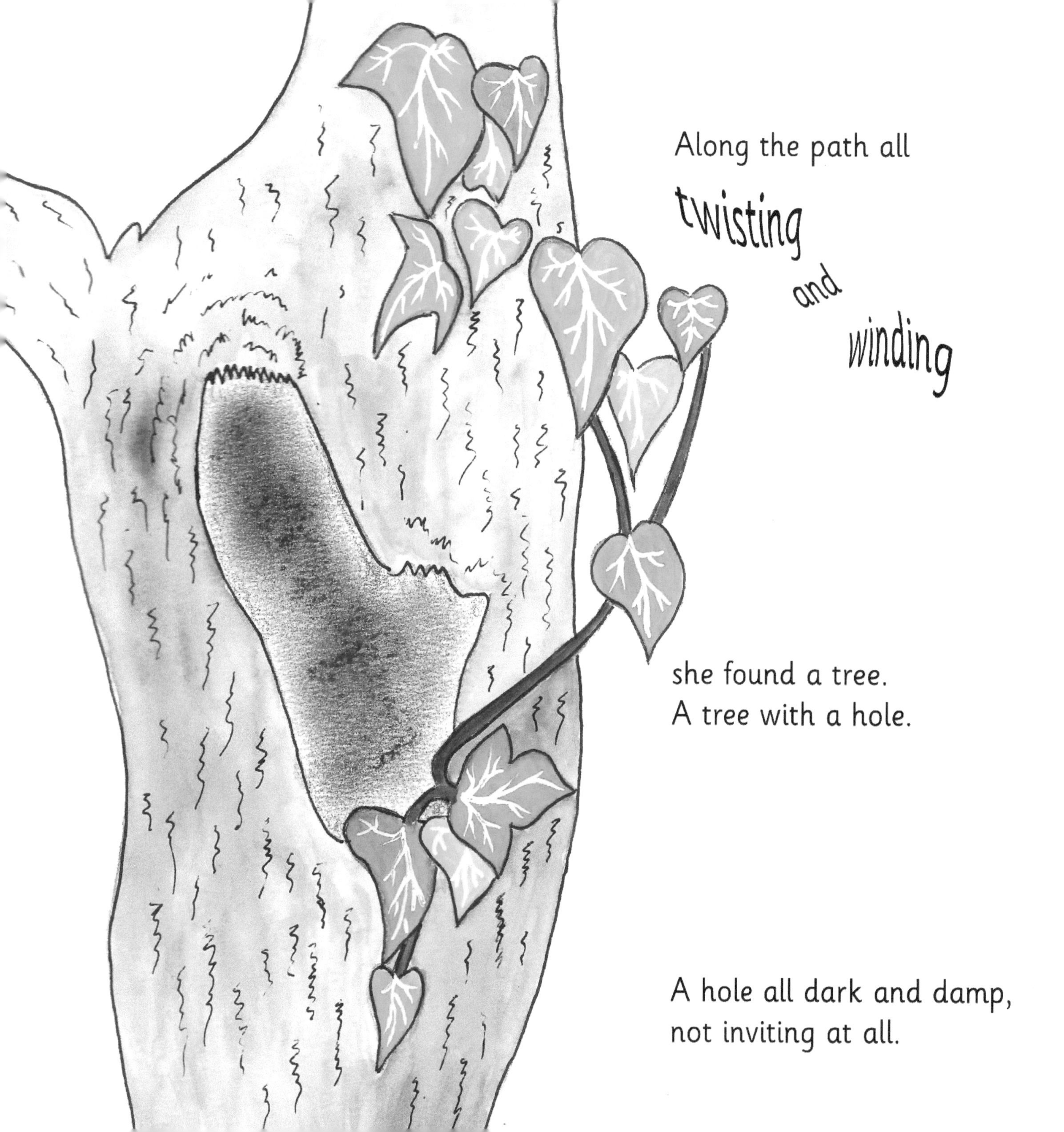

Along the path all
twisting
and
winding

she found a tree.
A tree with a hole.

A hole all dark and damp,
not inviting at all.

Little Lucy, small and shy, climbed UP and UP
to the hole all dark and damp.

A flash of black and white
and RED...

Not Magpie but Woodpecker.

Lucy sighed and said,
"Oh Woodpecker! Magpie stole my stone, my special stone that was bright and shiny, shining bright."

"It's little Lucy!" said Woodpecker.
"I remember you. Take one of my spotted feathers. If you need me. I will come."

Along the path all twisting and winding

Lucy found a clearing, "Is that a woodsman chopping trees?"
Little Lucy small and shy,
shy and small, no friends at all,
hid her face and slipped away.

Stepping back,
silently, silently.
Watch your step Lucy!

Lucy looked down,
hidden amongst the tall, tall grass,
a pheasant nest.

"1, 2, 3, 4, 5, 6, 7, 8, 9, 10 brown eggs.
Good job I didn't step on pheasant's eggs."

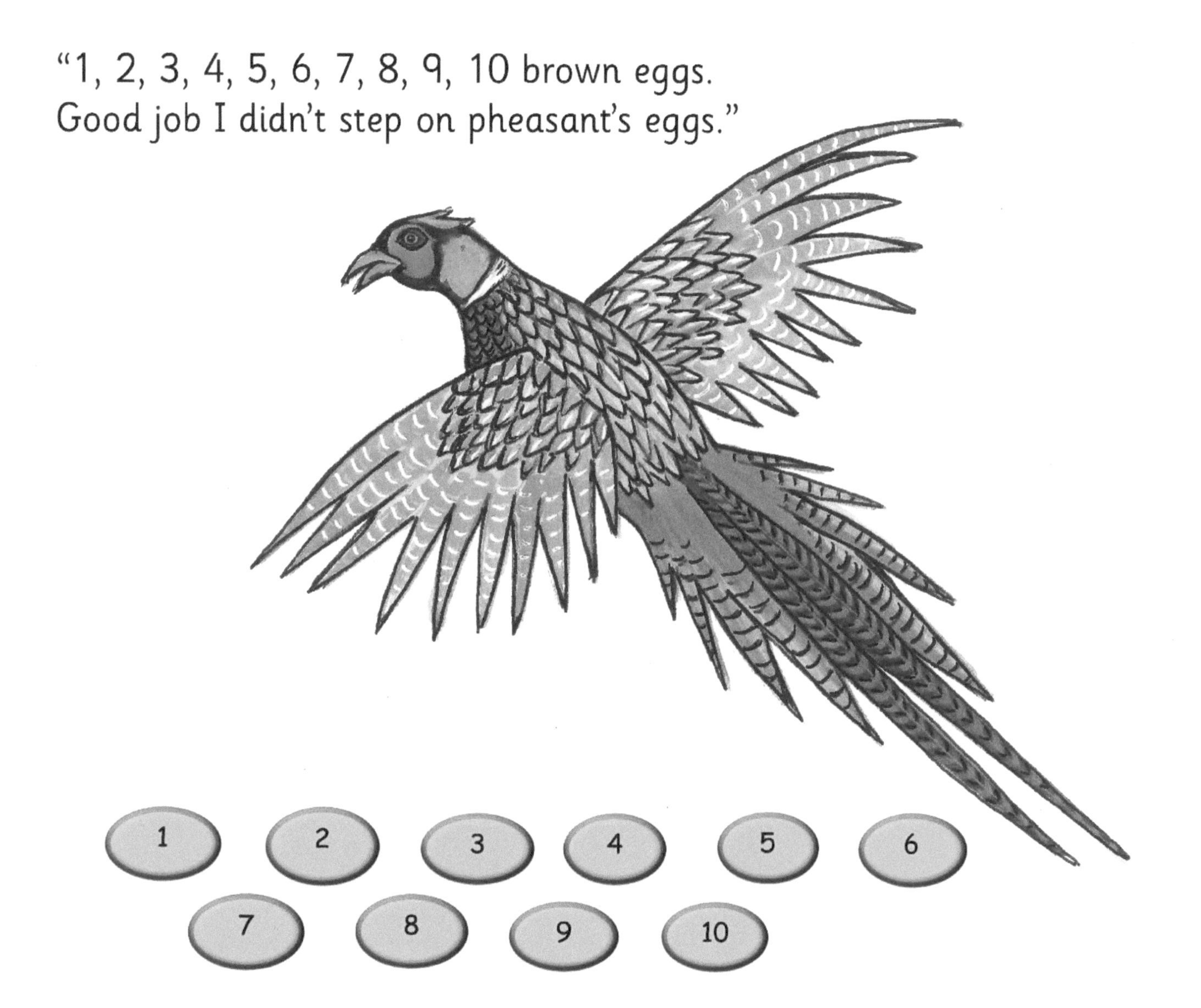

Lucy sighed and said, "Oh Pheasant! Magpie stole my stone, my special stone that was bright and shiny, shining bright."

"It's little Lucy!" said Pheasant. "I remember you. Take one of my long tail feathers. If you need me, I will come."

Plate 2

Look at the birds: they do not sow seeds, gather a harvest and put it in barns.

Yet your Father in Heaven takes care of them! Are you not worth much more than the birds?
Matthew 6:26

Down in the woodland
dim and dark
where the trees grew
thick and close,
a nest of sticks way up high,
stark against the sky.

"Time to be brave.

Time to be BIG not small".

Lucy climbed UP UP UP
to the nest of mud and sticks
balanced at the top.
Careful!

In the middle of Magpie's nest, a hoard of treasure.
Glistening and gleaming, sparkling and shimmering.
There,
shining bright
with its own special light
sat
little Lucy's stone.

Lucy took the stone,
her special stone
and held it tight.
"My treasure".

A flash of black and white, white and black.
Magpie swooped and shrieked,
pounced and pecked but...

Lucy ran and ran, down the tree,
through the clearing,
along the path all twisting

and

winding

past the tree with the hole, all dark and damp,
not inviting at all, past the ivy all tangled and twisted.

Magpie was not far behind, pouncing and pecking,
swooping and shrieking.
Lucy ran and ran.
She threw down Pheasant's feather.

Instantly, Pheasant was there,

flying UP, UP, UP.
Magpie was startled
and stopped awhile.

Magpie did not give up.
Lucy ran and ran.
She threw down Woodpecker's feather.

Instantly, Woodpecker was there.
Woodpecker pecked and pecked at Magpie.

Magpie still did not give up.
She swooped and shrieked, pounced and pecked.
Lucy ran and ran.
She threw down Robin's feather.

Where the feather fell ivy instanly grew with

winding,

twisting,

tangling stems.

Magpie was trapped.

Lucy stood still. All was quiet.
Holding the stone, shining bright,
she gazed again into the light,
and beheld the sight,
her face reflected in the light.

Robin, Woodpecker and Pheasant looked at Lucy
and saw her, truly saw her.
Little Lucy, small and shy, shy and small,
hiding her face from all.
But, not this time.

Brave and in control, Lucy stood up TALL.

Freeing Magpie from the twisting, tangled stems,
Lucy turned and left the stone, her special stone.
Left it, for Magpie.

"It's ME.
I did it!
I am Lucy.
I am BIG and TALL, not small.

I don't need to hide my face at all."

Plate 3 God knows your name!

I have called you by name, you are mine. *Isaiah 43:1.*

Even the hairs of your head have all been counted. *Luke 12:7*

And I will be with you always, to the end of the age. *Matthew 28:20*

The End

Nature Notes

Did you spot all these in the story? Can you go back and name them?

IVY: An evergreen plant that can climb up walls and trees (green leaves are present throughout the year). The leaves are glossy with pale veins. Ivy provides homes for many insects, and a safe place for birds to build nests. The pale greenish flowers are an important source of nectar for insects through the Autumn.

MAGPIE: Magpies are intelligent birds belonging to the crow family. Legend suggests they have a fondness for shiny objects and steal them to take back to their nest. They eat a variety of foods: insects, fruits, berries, seeds, and small mammals (e.g. mice). They will raid the nests of smaller birds and take the eggs or young.

ROBIN: Also known as Robin Redbreast. They are friendly birds, often following a gardener to find disturbed insects or worms. The first postmen wore bright red coats and so Victorian postmen were nick-named 'Robins'. Sending cards at Christmas became popular and when postment - Robins - delivered them, the bird became associated with Christmas.

GREAT SPOTTED WOODPECKER: Often seen clinging to tree trunks. It uses its strong beak to drill nest holes out of the tree trunk, and to search for insects under the bark of the tree. In Spring it can be heard drumming on tree trunks to attract a mate and to claim a territory.

PHEASANT: Pheasants are often seen in fields and in woodland where there is plenty of cover, nesting mostly on the ground. Originally from Asia, they were introduced to the UK back in history possibly by the Romans.

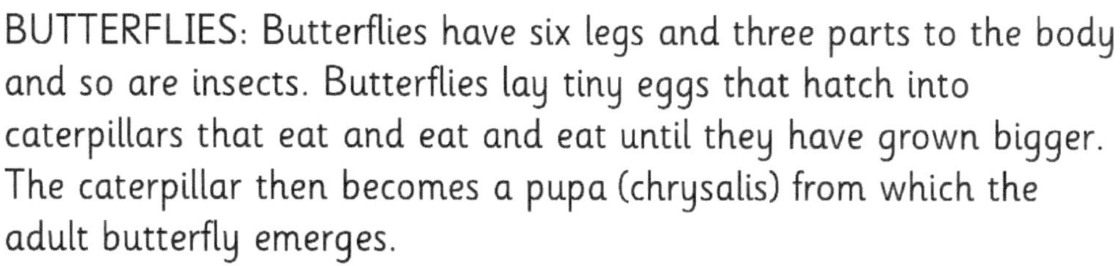

BUTTERFLIES: Butterflies have six legs and three parts to the body and so are insects. Butterflies lay tiny eggs that hatch into caterpillars that eat and eat and eat until they have grown bigger. The caterpillar then becomes a pupa (chrysalis) from which the adult butterfly emerges.
HOLLY BLUE BUTTERFLY: Food plants: holly and ivy.
RED ADMIRAL BUTTERFLY: Food plant: nettles.

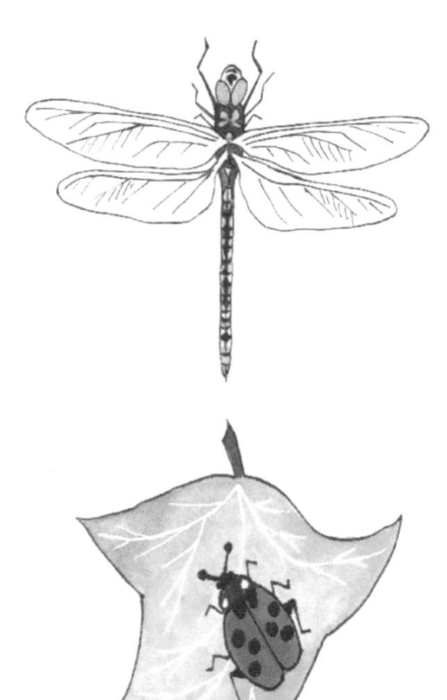

SOUTHERN HAWKER DRAGONFLY: Dragonflies are also insects. They do not breathe fire or sting; despite being called dragons! They are fast at flying, catching other insects in the air. Females lay eggs in freshwater and the young dragonflies (Nymphs) can spend several years in the water feeding and growing. Like the adults, they are also fierce carnivores. Nymphs climb out of the pond and the adult winged dragonflies emerge. Dragonflies can be curious. If you stand still by a pond where they are flying, they may come and have a close look at you too!

7-SPOTTED LADYBIRD: Ladybirds also have six legs and three parts to the body and so are insects. Their front wings are hardened into a shell-like wing-case, so they are a type of insect called beetles. Ladybirds eat greenfly and blackfly (aphids) making them popular with gardeners. Their bright colours are a warning to birds that they taste horrible!

COMMON LIZARD: Lizards are reptiles. They are cold-blooded, meaning they cannot maintain a warm body temperature without taking in heat from outside. They can often be seen sunbathing or basking in the warm sun to reach a body temperature at which they can be active.

Lightning Source UK Ltd.
Milton Keynes UK
UKHW050917060921
390004UK00002B/37
* 9 7 8 1 9 1 3 9 4 6 7 5 3 *